LITTLE SCHOLARZ

NUMBERS
WRITING BOOK
1 to 100

NAME _______________________

CLASS ____________ SEC. ________

SCHOOL _______________________

____

LITTLE SCHOLARZ PVT. LTD.

1

ONE

☀ Trace and write:

Date: ....

Teacher's signature: ....

2

☀ Trace and write:

2

3

THREE

☀ Trace and write:

3   3   3   3   3   3   3   3

Date: .... Teacher's signature: ....

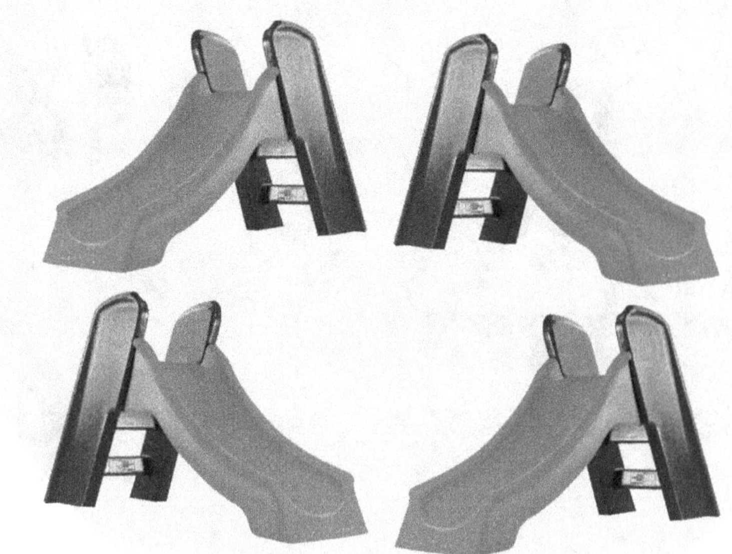

☼ Trace and write:

4 | 4 4 4 4 4 4 4

Date: .... Teacher's signature: ....

5

FIVE

☼ Trace and write:

Date: ....

Teacher's signature: ....

6

SIX

☀ Trace and write:

Date: ....

Teacher's signature: ....

7

SEVEN

☼ Trace and write:

Date: ....

Teacher's signature: ....

8
EIGHT

☼ Trace and write:

8 8 8 8 8 8 8

Date: ....   Teacher's signature: ....

☀ # Trace and write:

Date: ....   Teacher's signature: ....

IO

TEN

☼ Trace and write:

Date: ....

Teacher's signature: ....

ADD

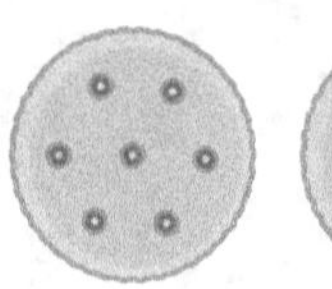 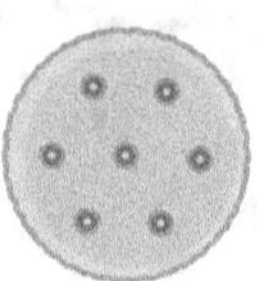 **+** 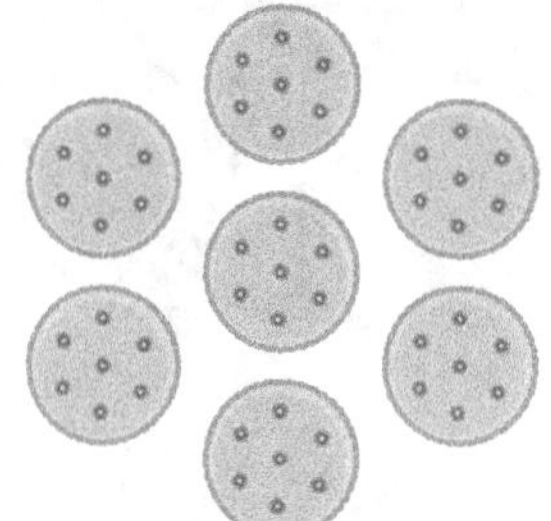 **=** 

 **+**  **=** 

 **+**  **=** 

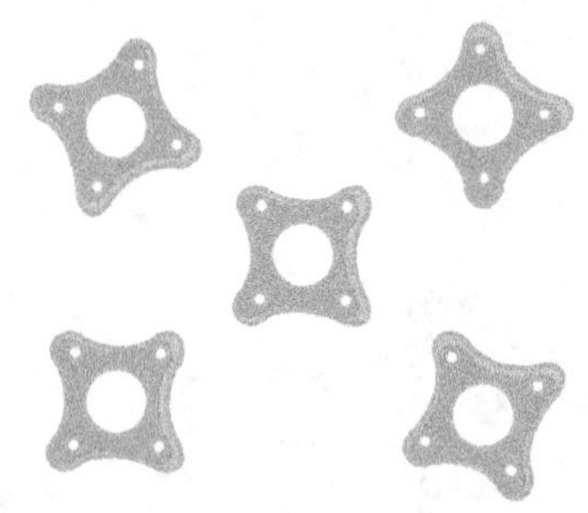 **+** 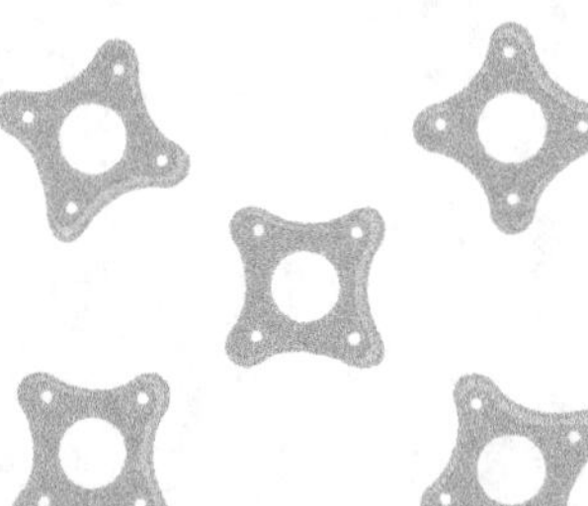 **=** 

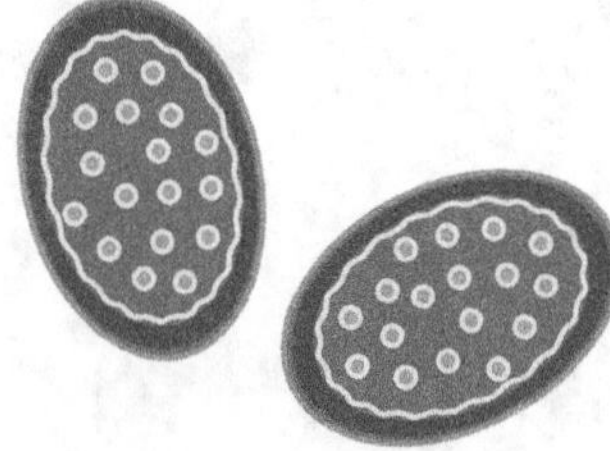 **+** 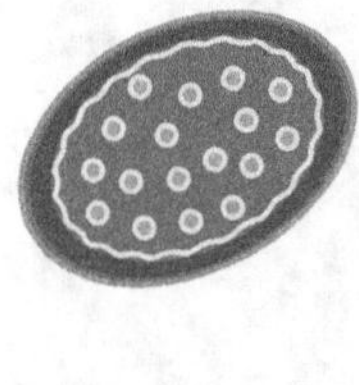 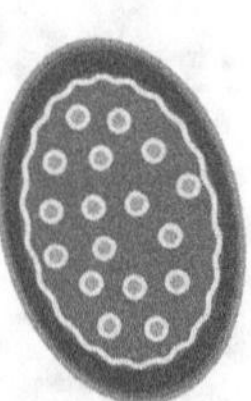 **=** 

Date: ....

Teacher's signature: ....

Count and write the number of pictures in the given boxes:

Date: ....

Teacher's signature: ....

☀ ## Circle the correct number:

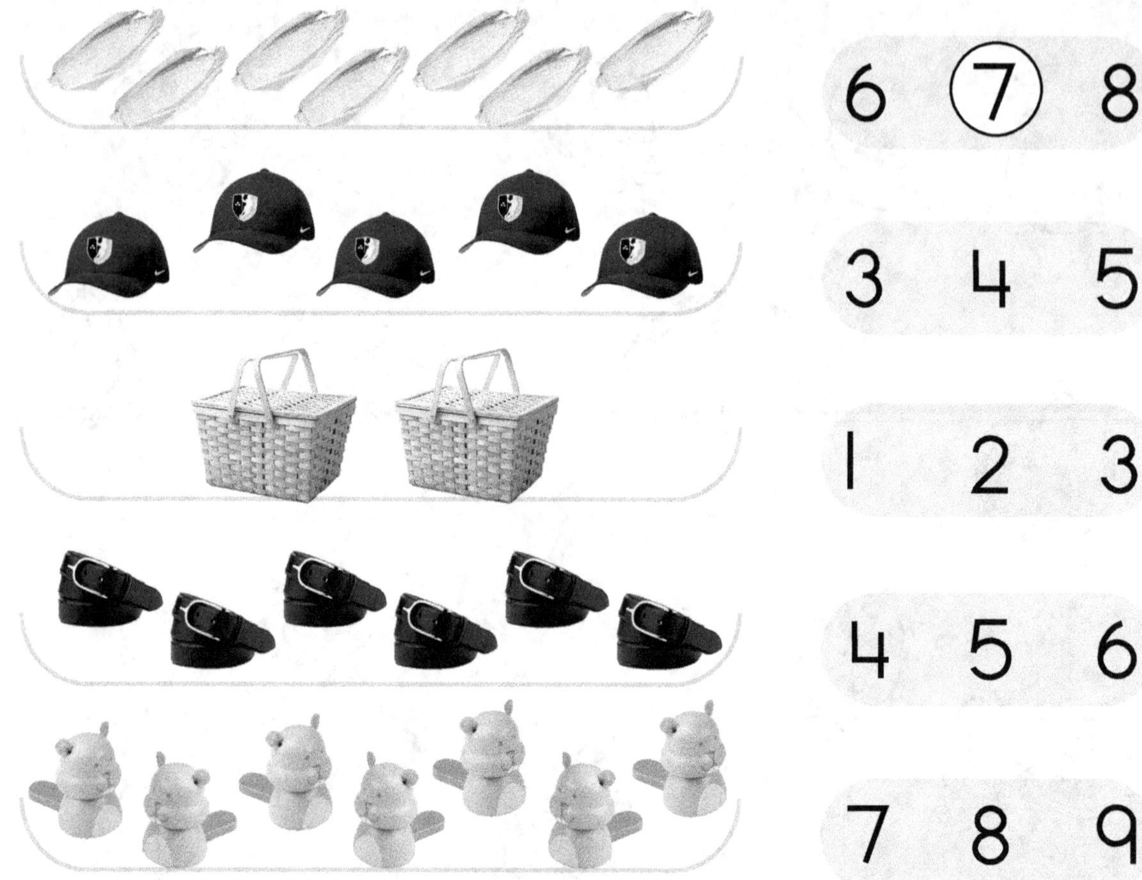

	6 ⑦ 8
	3 4 5
	1 2 3
	4 5 6
	7 8 9

☀ ## Trace the number names and write in figures:

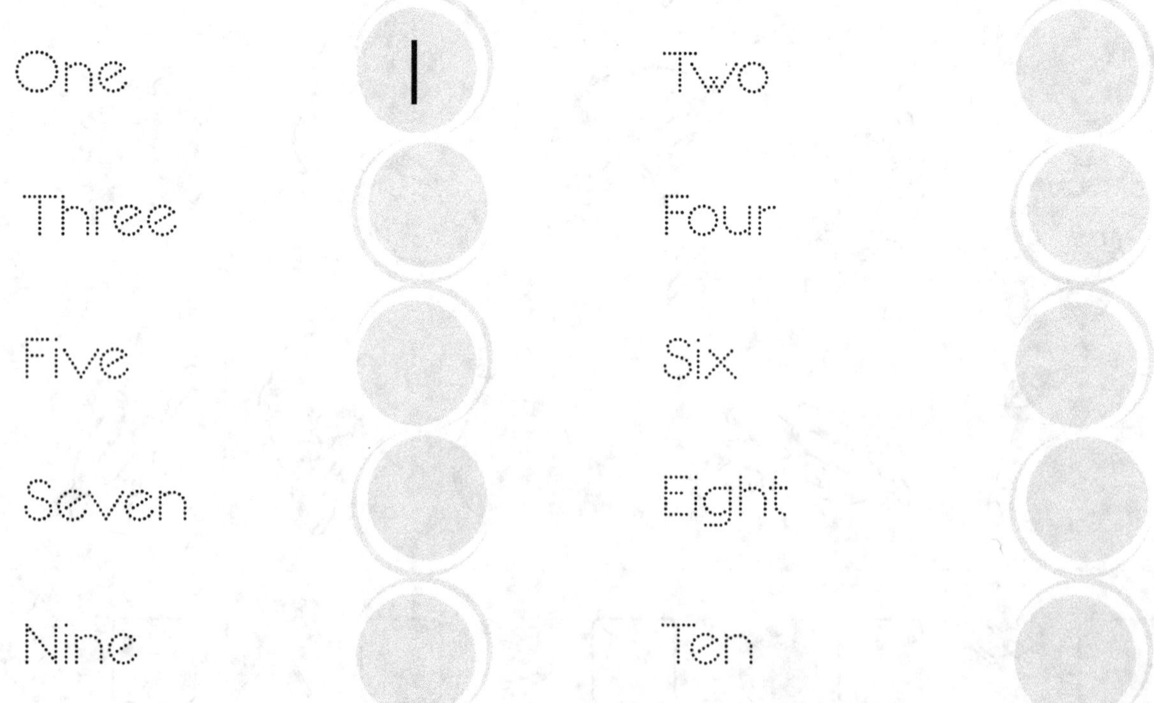

One	1	Two	
Three		Four	
Five		Six	
Seven		Eight	
Nine		Ten	

☼ Trace and write:

Date: ....   Teacher's signature: ....

TWELVE

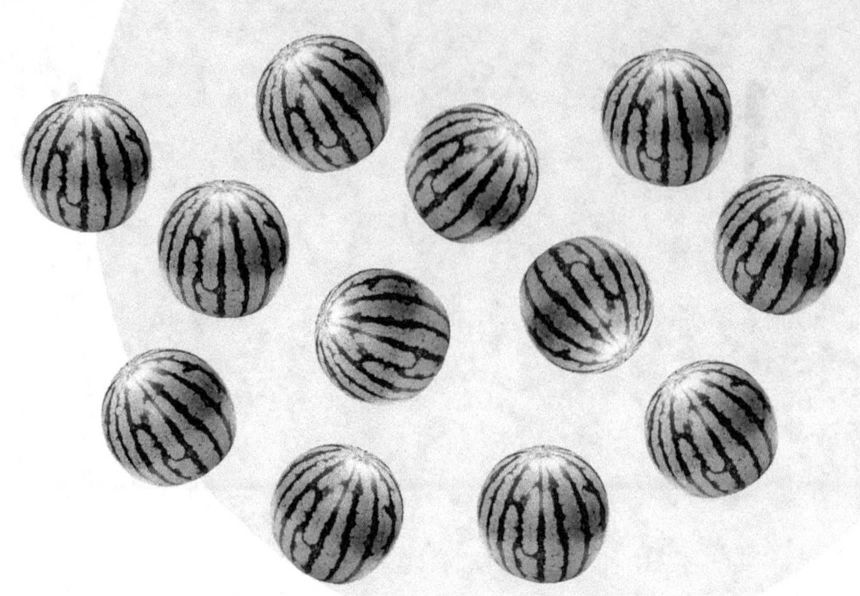

☼ Trace and write:

12	12 12 12 12 12 12 12 12

12

12

12

12

12

Date: ....   Teacher's signature: ....

13

THIRTEEN

☀ Trace and write:

13

13 13 13 13 13 13 13 13

13
13
13
13
13
13

☀ Trace and write:

Date: .... Teacher's signature: ....

☀ Trace and write:

15 15 15 15 15 15 15 15 15

15

15

15

15

15

15

Date: ....

Teacher's signature: ....

16

SIXTEEN

☀ Trace and write:

16

16 16 16 16 16 16

16

16

16

16

16

Date: ....

Teacher's signature: ....

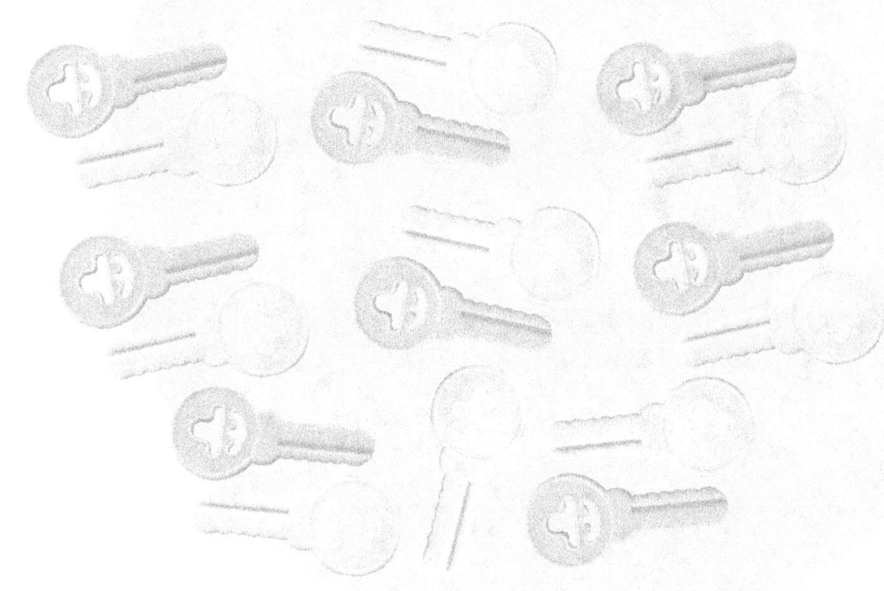

☼ Trace and write:

Date: ....

Teacher's signature: ....

18

☀ Trace and write:

18 | 18 18 18 18 18 18 18

18
18
18
18
18

NINETEEN

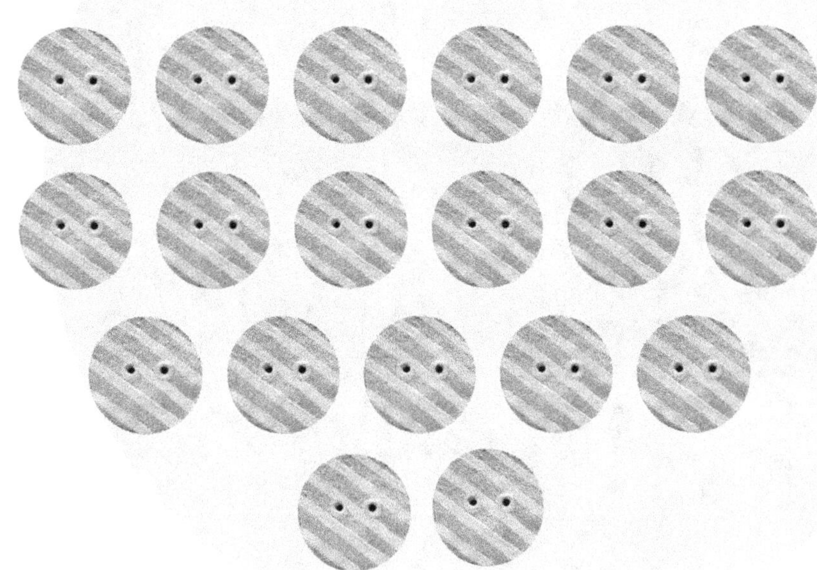

☀ Trace and write:

Date: ....

Teacher's signature: ....

20

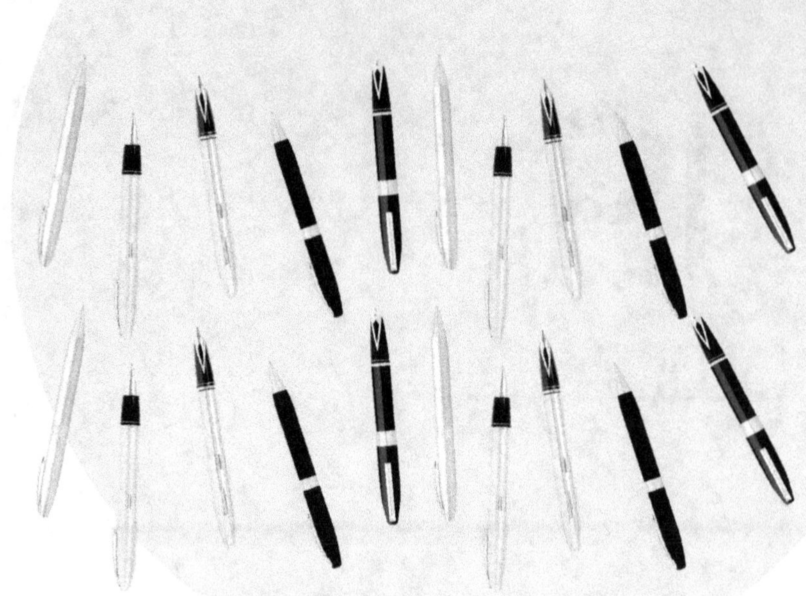

☀ Trace and write:

20

Date: ....

Teacher's signature: ....

☀ Write the correct number:

Between	Before	After

Between

11 (12) 13

13 ◯ 15

15 ◯ 17

16 ◯ 18

18 ◯ 20

Before

(19) 20

◯ 13

◯ 15

◯ 18

◯ 19

After

11 (12)

10 ◯

14 ◯

16 ◯

19 ◯

☀ Trace the number names and write in figures:

Eleven   11   Twelve

Thirteen   Fourteen

Fifteen   Sixteen

Seventeen   Eighteen

Nineteen   Twenty

TAKE AWAY

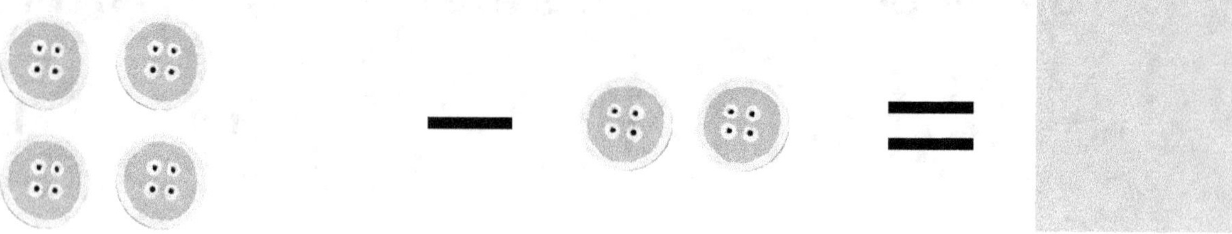

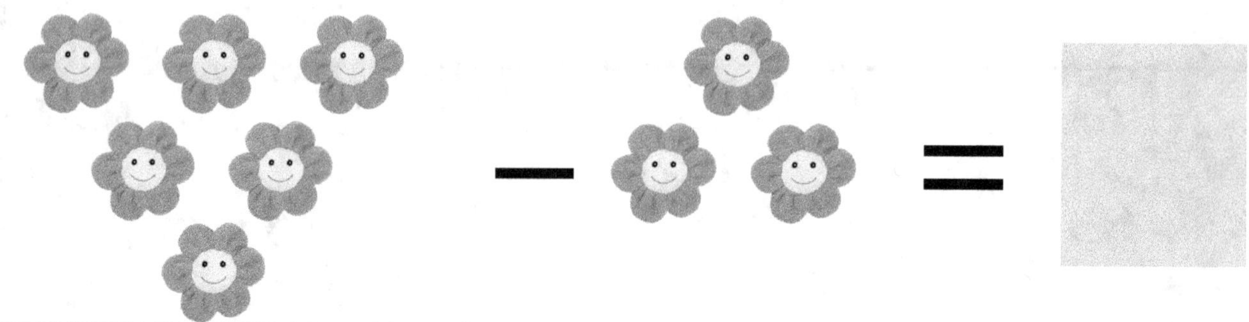

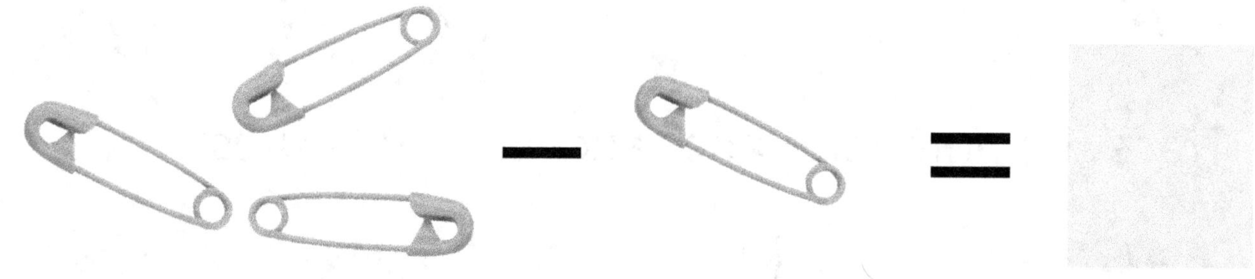

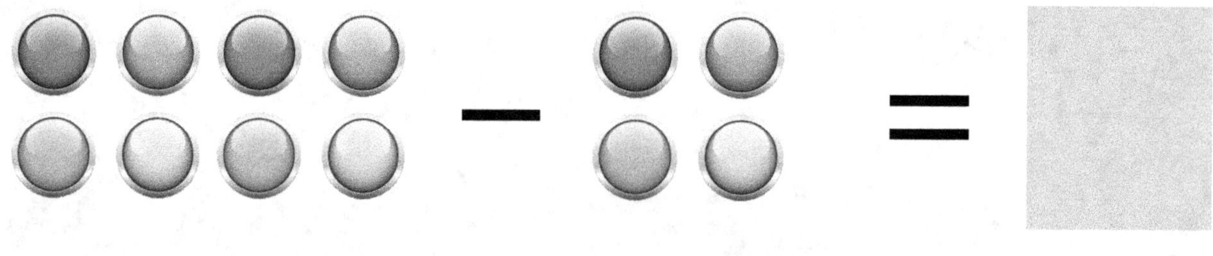

Count and write the number:

 11

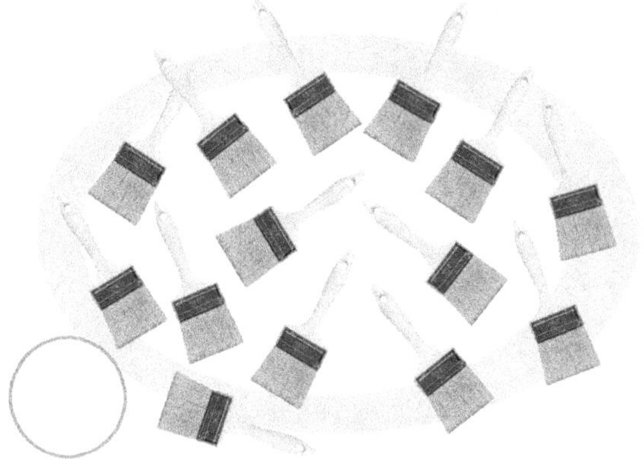

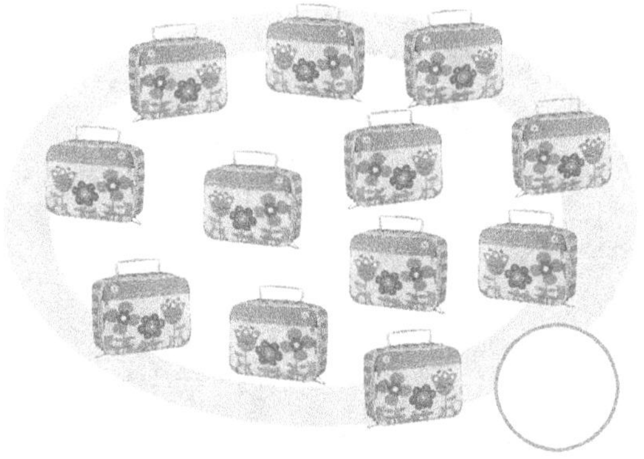

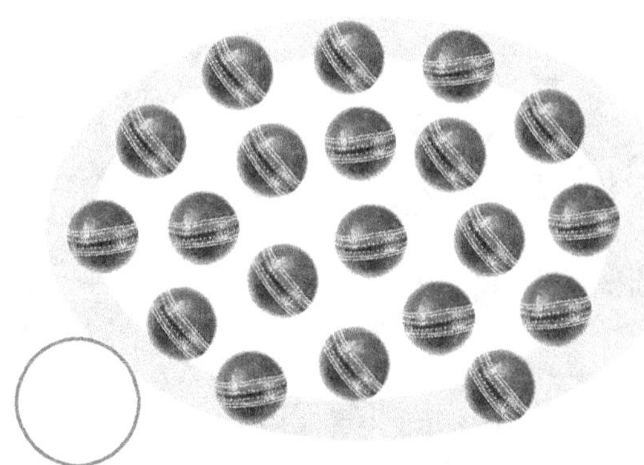

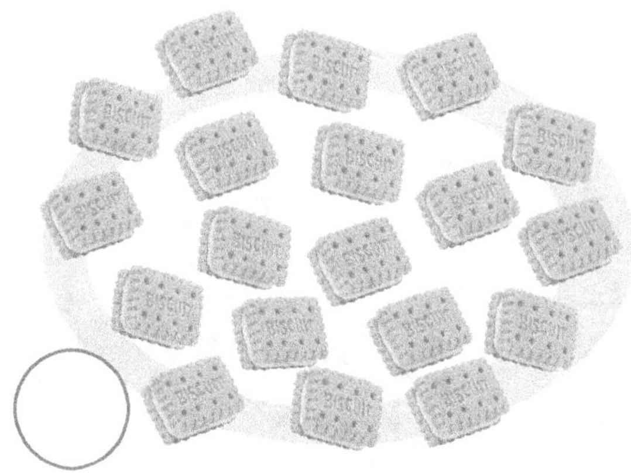

Date: .... Teacher's signature: ....

21
TWENTY ONE

TO

25
TWENTY FIVE

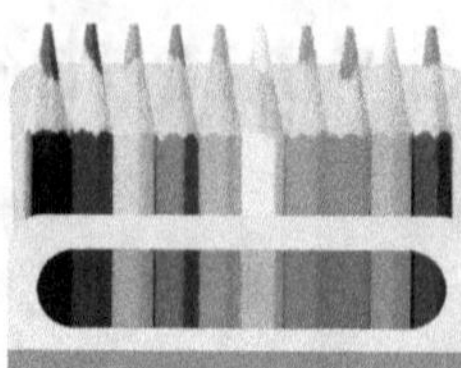
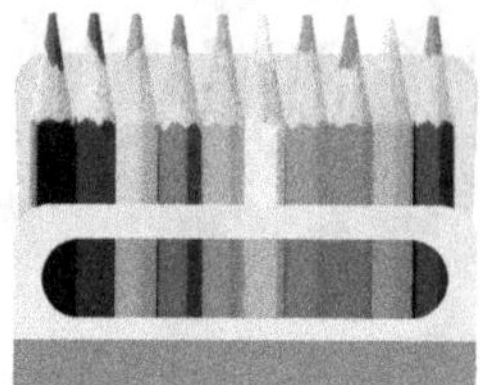
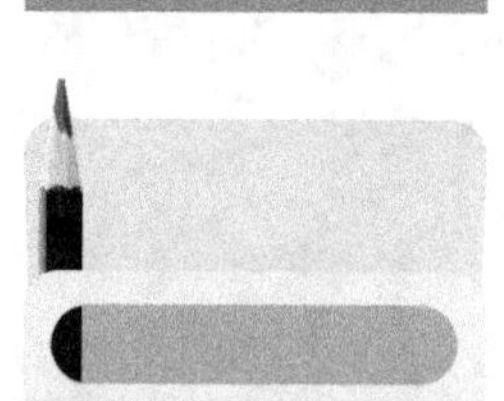
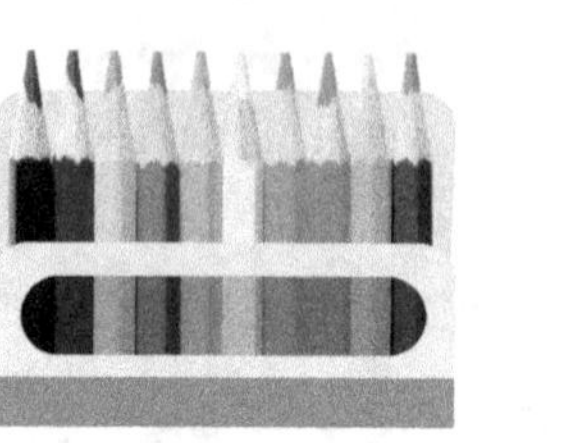

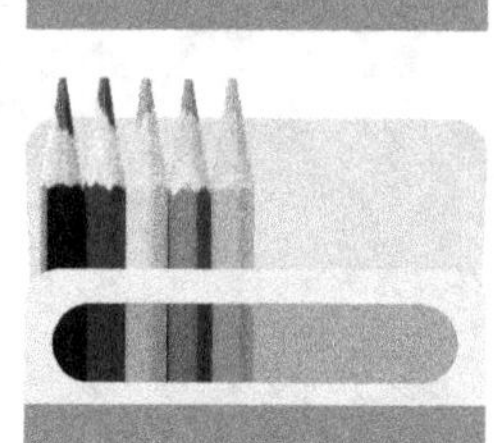

21	21	21	21	21
22	22	22	22	22
23	23	23	23	23
24	24	24	24	24
25	25	25	25	25

Date: ....

Teacher's signature: ....

26
TWENTY SIX

TO

30
THIRTY

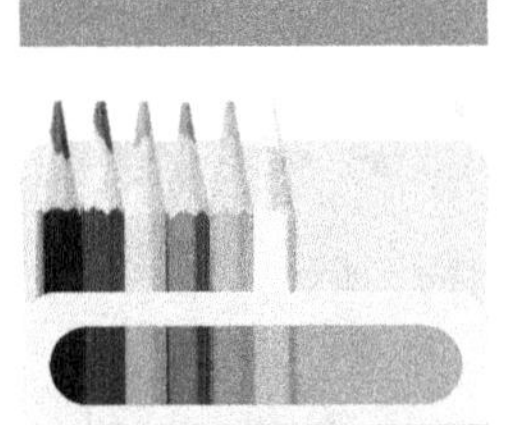

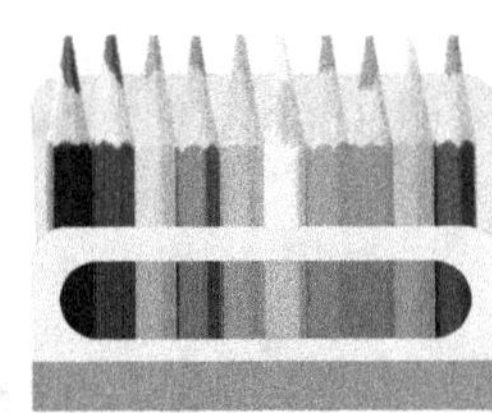

26	26	26	26	26
27	27	27	27	27
28	28	28	28	28
29	29	29	29	29
30	30	30	30	30

Date: ....

Teacher's signature: ....

☀ Write the correct number:

Between	Before	After
21 (22) 23	(26) 27	21 (22)
26 ◯ 28	◯ 22	29 ◯
22 ◯ 24	◯ 30	23 ◯
20 ◯ 22	◯ 28	27 ◯
28 ◯ 30	◯ 24	24 ◯

☀ Circle (◯) the smaller number in each group:

10 (2)	17 22	14 9
11 22	30 25	3 4
2 3 4	5 1 8	19 21 7
20 11 10	3 5 6	4 17 8
22 25 30	18 12 15	23 16 14

Date: ....   Teacher's signature: ....

(7)   6   12   16   10   8

  2   5   6   10   13   20

  10 6 7   20 11 12   25 16 23

  26 21 30   15 20 10   14 19 16

  17 12 13   22 24 21   3   7   5

☀ Colour the shapes and match the numbers:

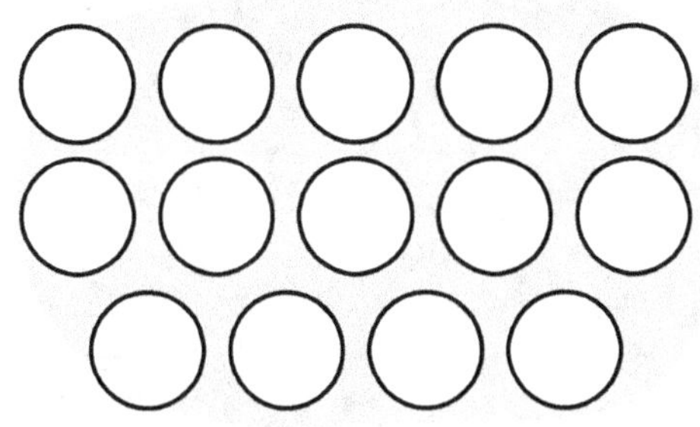

25

20

22

14

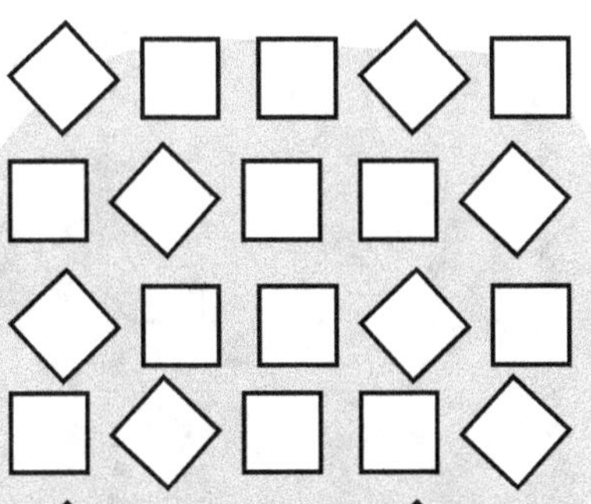

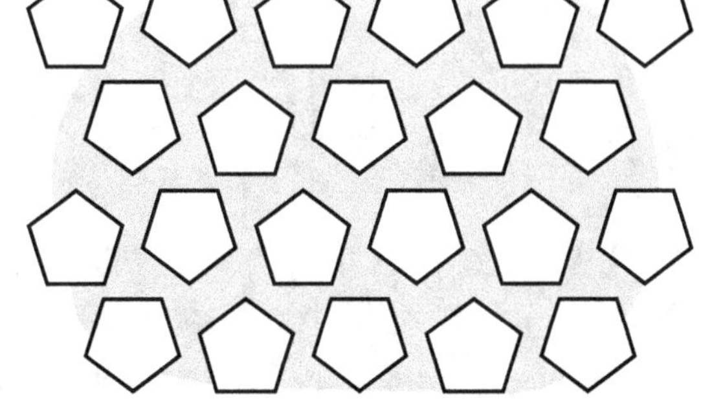

31
THIRTY ONE

TO

35
THIRTY FIVE

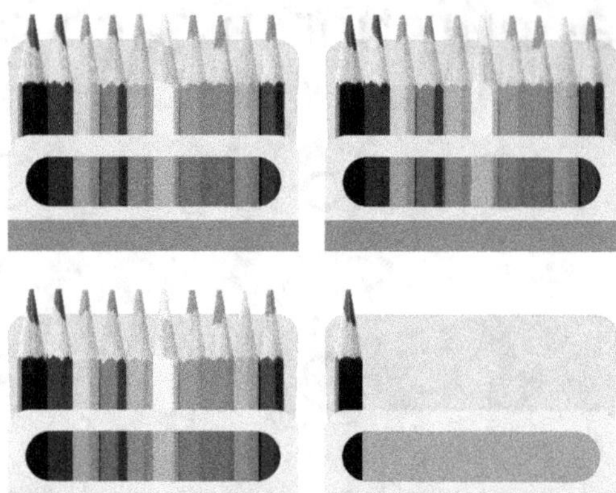

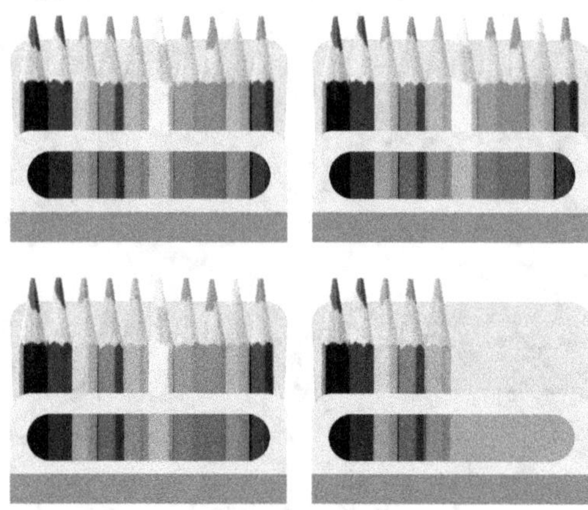

31	31	31	31	31
32	32	32	32	32
33	33	33	33	33
34	34	34	34	34
35	35	35	35	35

Date: ....

Teacher's signature: ....

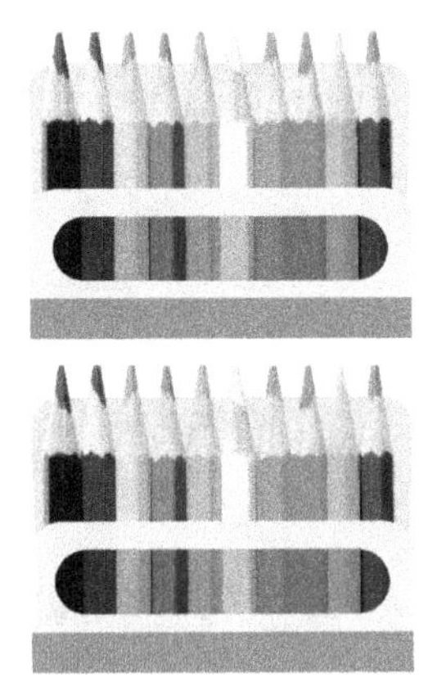
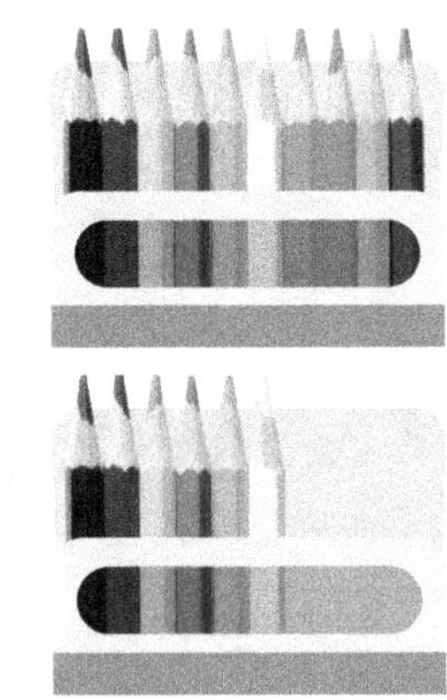
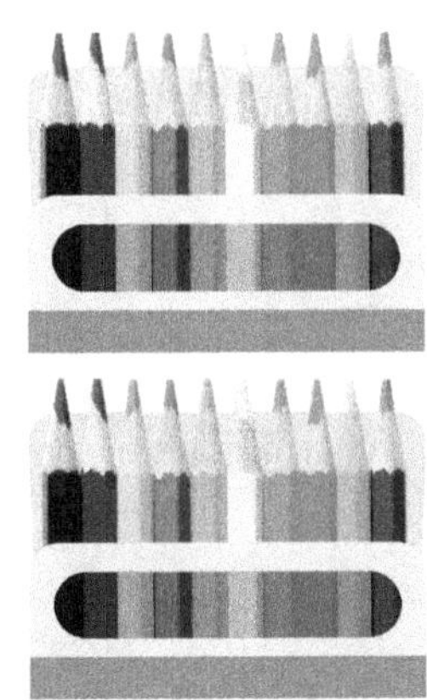
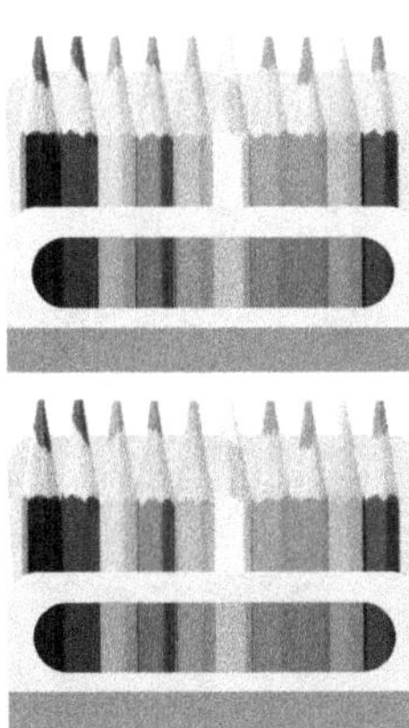

36	36	36	36	36
37	37	37	37	37
38	38	38	38	38
39	39	39	39	39
40	40	40	40	40

Date: ....

Teacher's signature: ....

☀ Write the next three numbers:

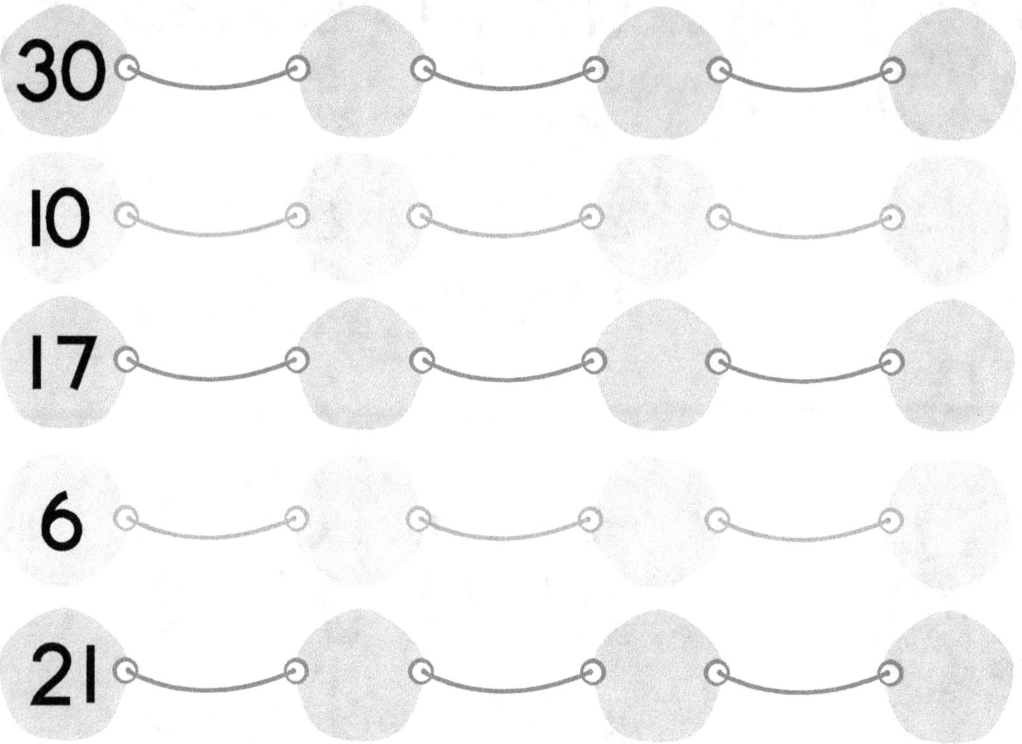

30

10

17

6

21

☀ Arrange these numbers from smallest to greatest:

33   34   30   31

21   20   22   12

10   14   11   36

☀ Trace the number names and write in figures:

Thirty One — 31   Thirty Two

Thirty Three   Thirty Four

Thirty Five   Thirty Six

Thirty Seven   Thirty Eight

Thirty Nine   Forty

☀ Write the missing numbers:

			4			7			10
11				15					20
21							28		30
31		33			36				40

Date: ....   Teacher's signature: ....

41

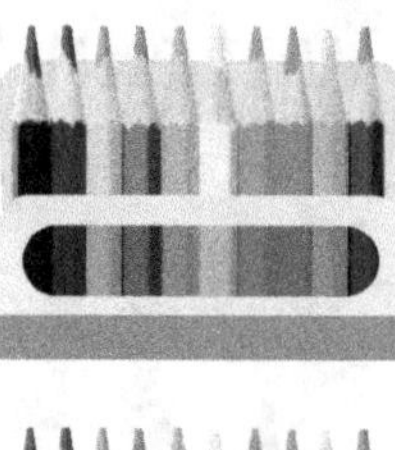
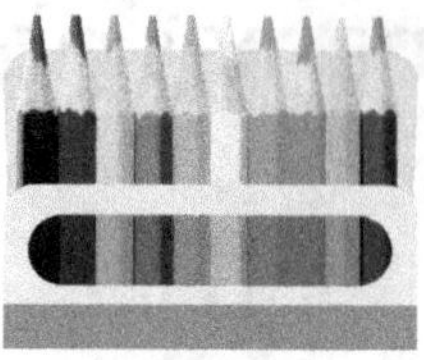

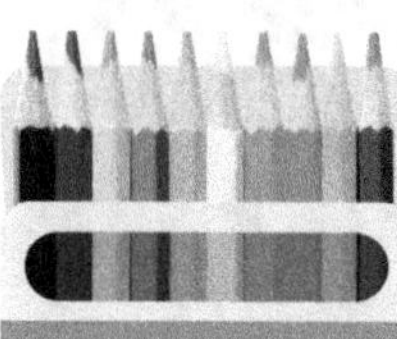

FORTY ONE

TO

45

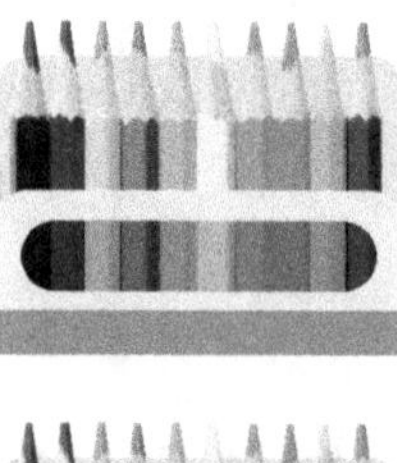

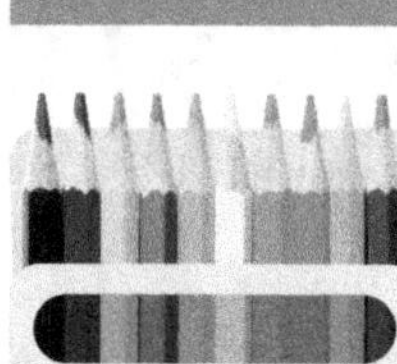

FORTY FIVE

41	41	41	41	41
42	42	42	42	42
43	43	43	43	43
44	44	44	44	44
45	45	45	45	45

Date: ....

Teacher's signature: ....

46

TO

50

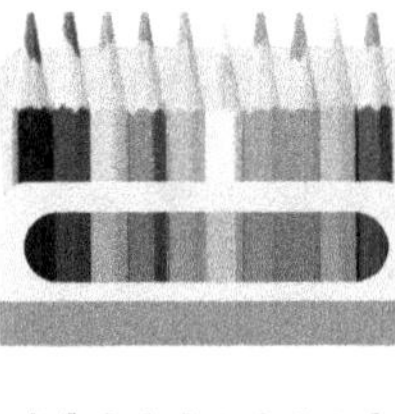
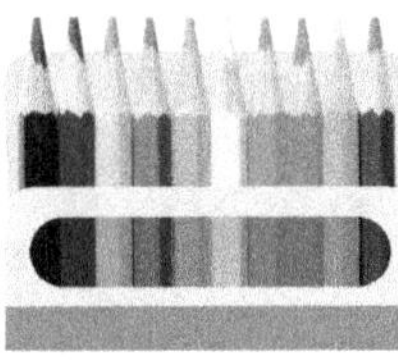

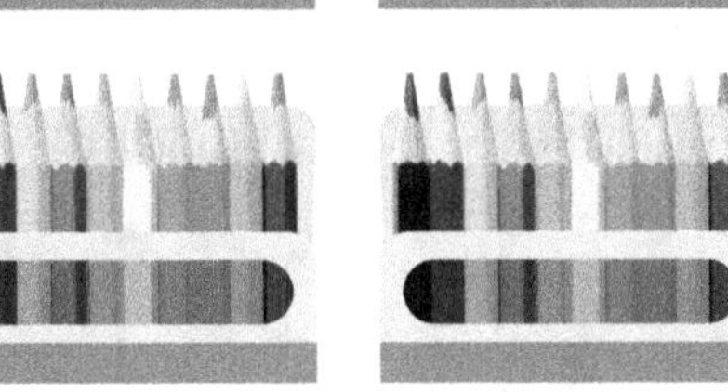

46	46	46	46	46
47	47	47	47	47
48	48	48	48	48
49	49	49	49	49
50	50	50	50	50

Date: ....

Teacher's signature: ....

41   41

42   42

43   43

44   44

45   45

46   46

47   47

48   48

49   49

50   50

Date: ....   (38)   Teacher's signature: ....

Count the pencils and write in the box:

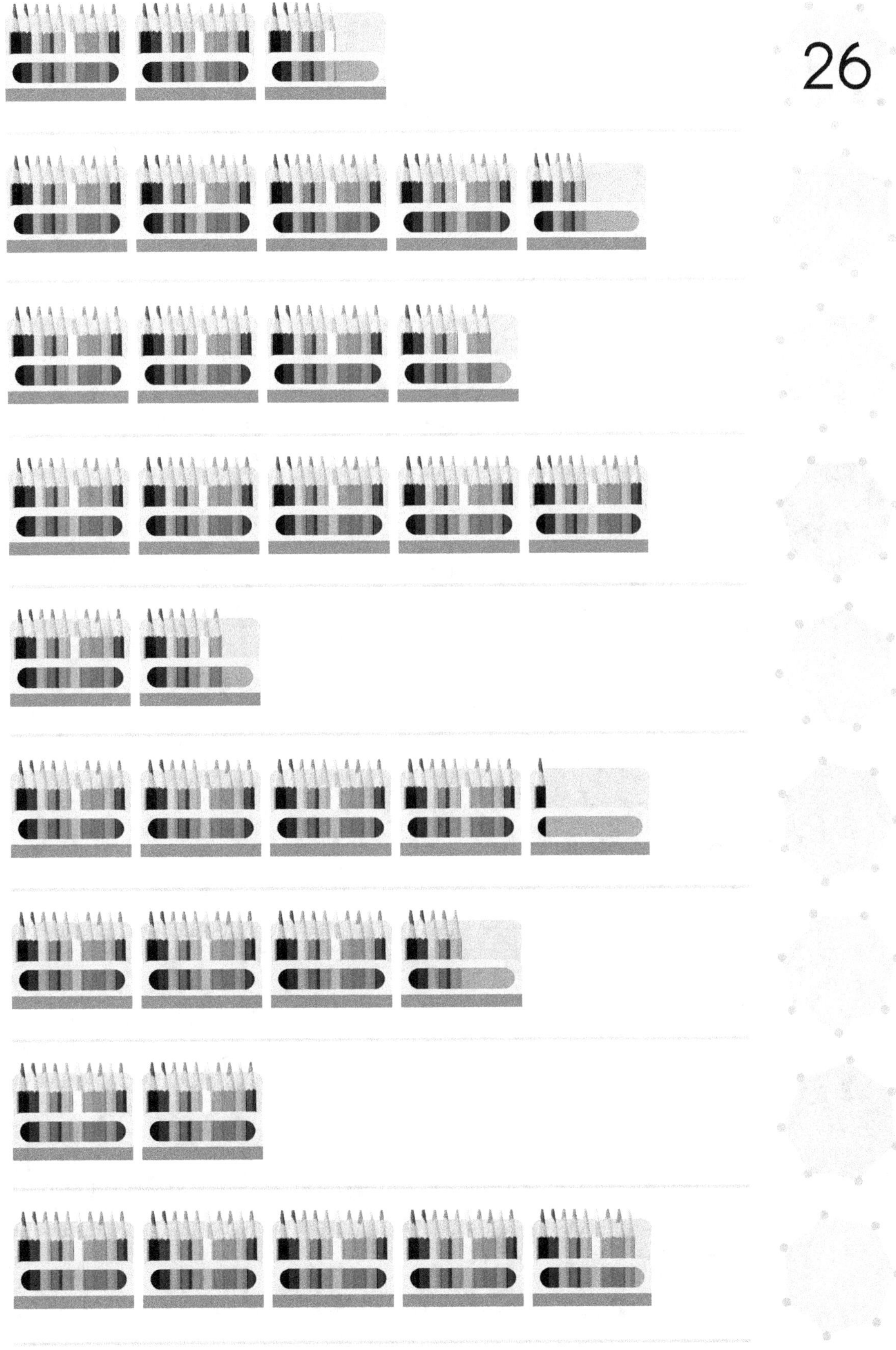

26

Date: ....

Teacher's signature: ....

51

TO

55

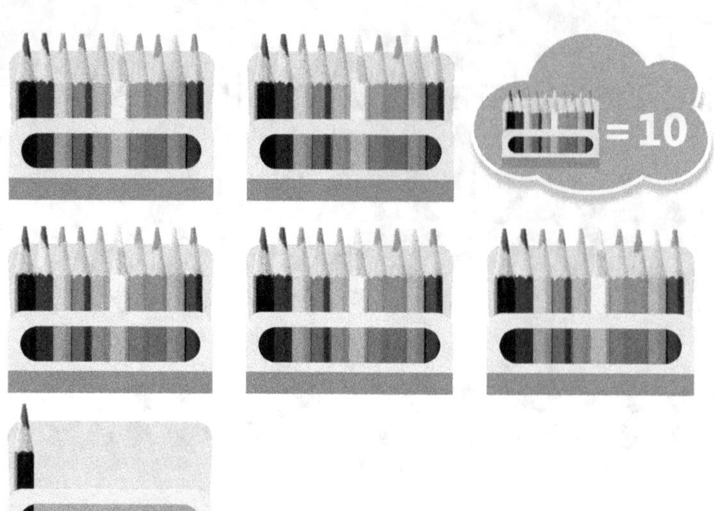

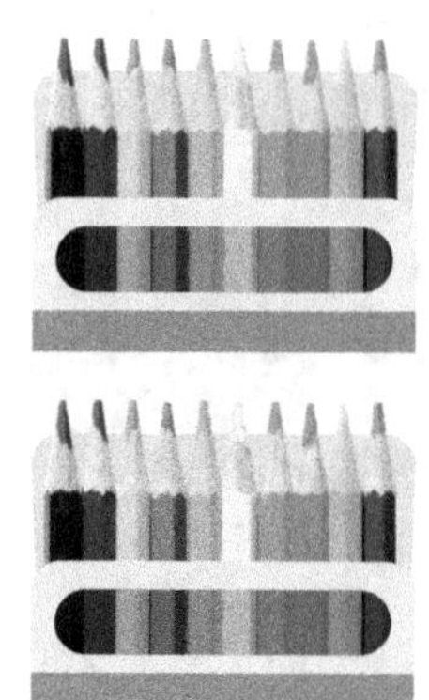
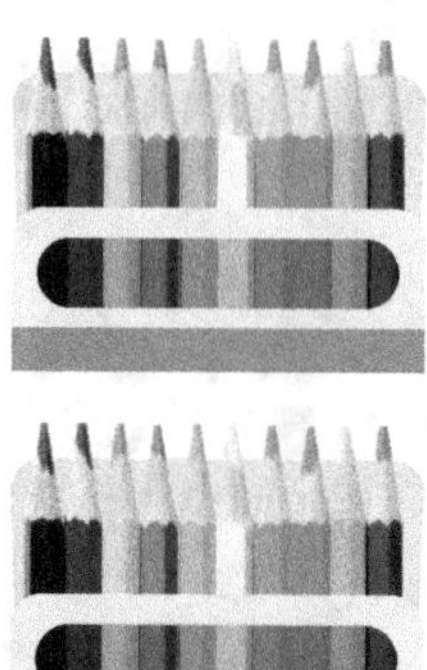
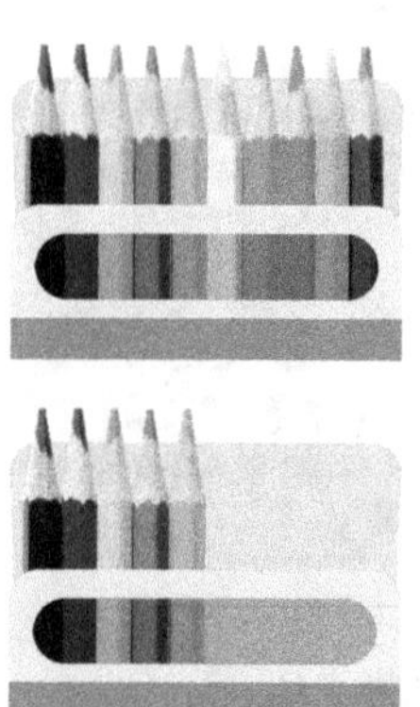

51		51	51	51	51
52		52	52	52	52
53		53	53	53	53
54		54	54	54	54
55		55	55	55	55

Date: ....

Teacher's signature: ....

56
FIFTY SIX

TO

60
SIXTY

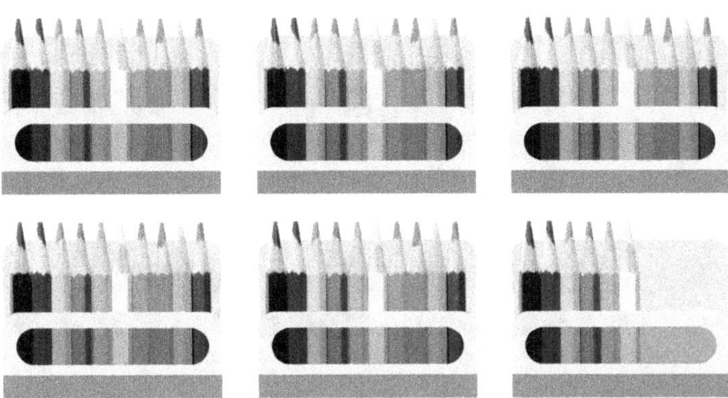

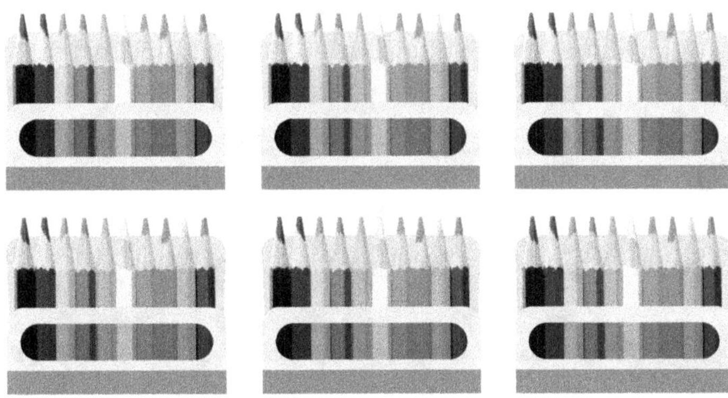

56	56	56	56	56
57	57	57	57	57
58	58	58	58	58
59	59	59	59	59
60	60	60	60	60

Date: ....   Teacher's signature: ....

61

SIXTY ONE

TO

65

SIXTY FIVE

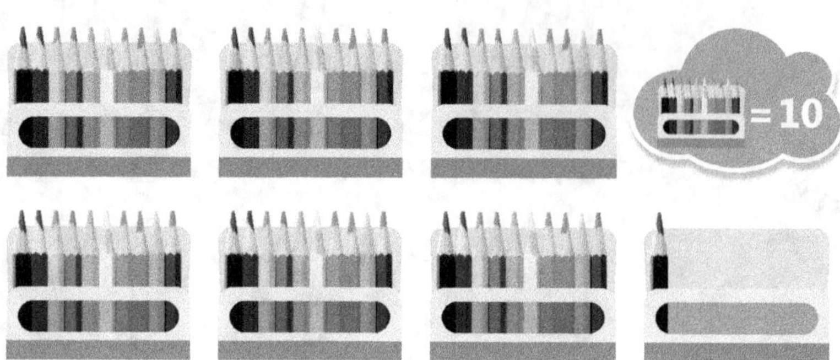

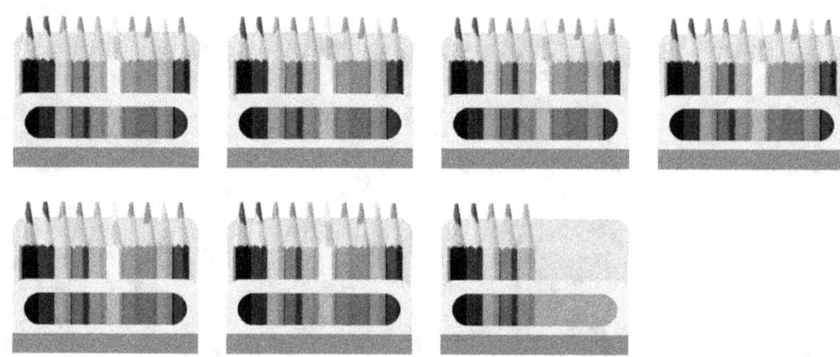

61	61	61	61	61
62	62	62	62	62
63	63	63	63	63
64	64	64	64	64
65	65	65	65	65

Date: ....

Teacher's signature: ....

66

SIXTY SIX

TO

70

SEVENTY

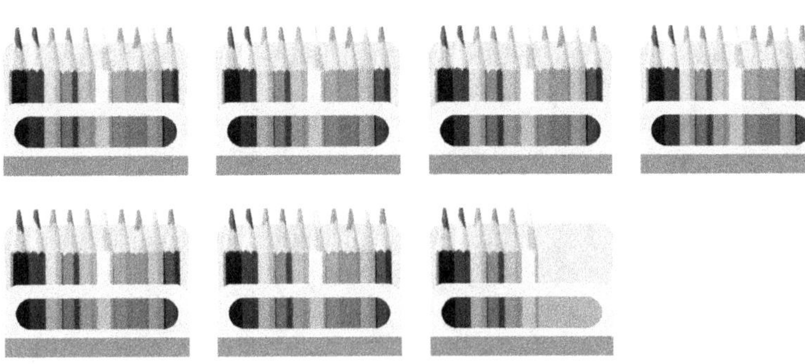

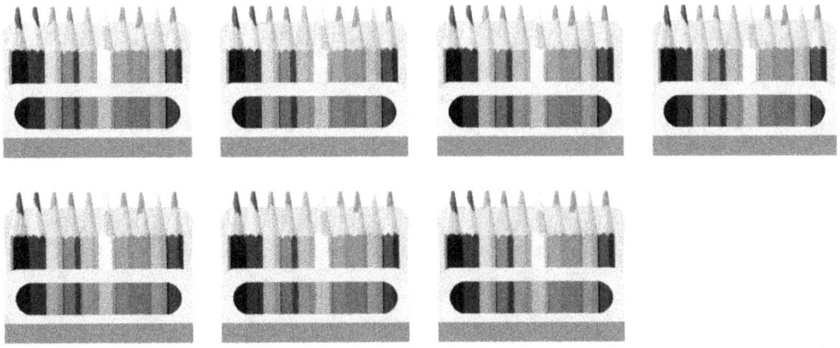

66		66		66		66		66	
67		67		67		67		67	
68		68		68		68		68	
69		69		69		69		69	
70		70		70		70		70	

Date: ....

Teacher's signature: ....

Write the numbers from 51 to 60:

51   51
52   52
53   53
54   54
55   55
56   56
57   57
58   58
59   59
60   60

Date: ....

Teacher's signature: ....

61
62
63
64
65
66
67
68
69
70

71

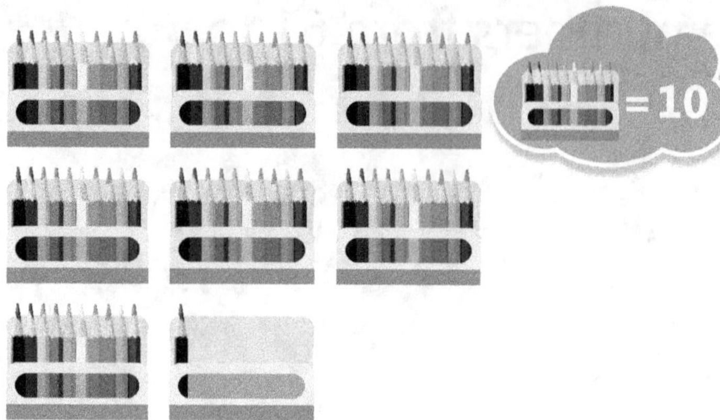

TO

75

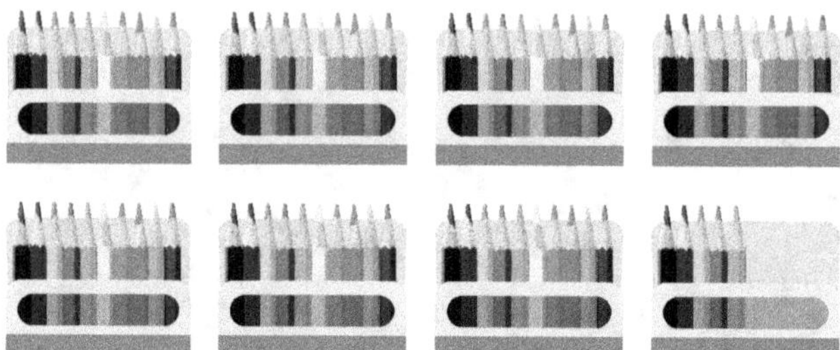

71	71	71	71	71
72	72	72	72	72
73	73	73	73	73
74	74	74	74	74
75	75	75	75	75

Date: ....

Teacher's signature: ....

76

TO

80

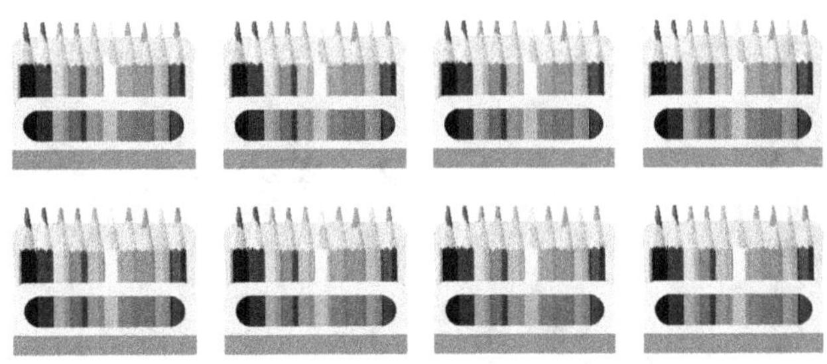

76	76	76	76	76
77	77	77	77	77
78	78	78	78	78
79	79	79	79	79
80	80	80	80	80

Date: ....　　　Teacher's signature: ....

81

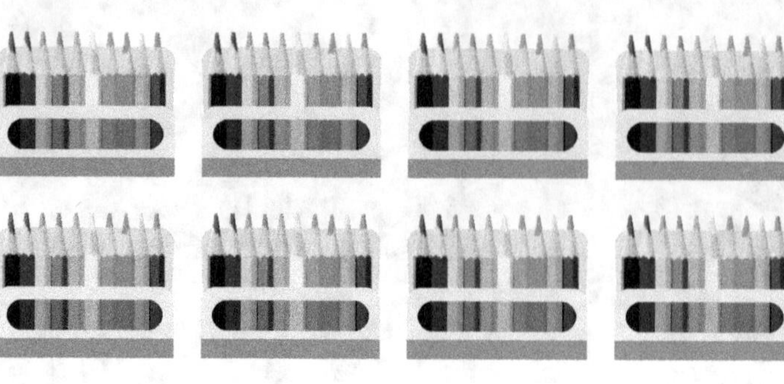

TO

85

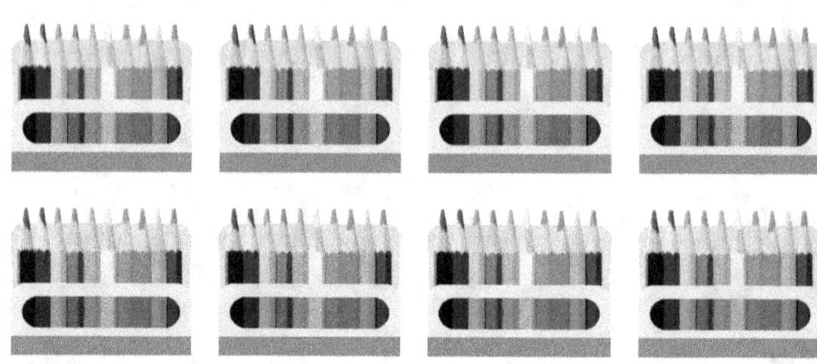
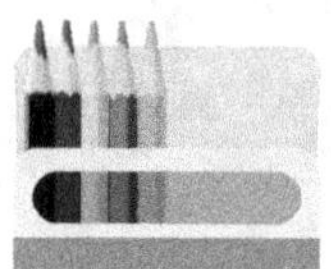

81	81	81	81	81
82	82	82	82	82
83	83	83	83	83
84	84	84	84	84
85	85	85	85	85

Date: ....

Teacher's signature: ....

86

TO

90

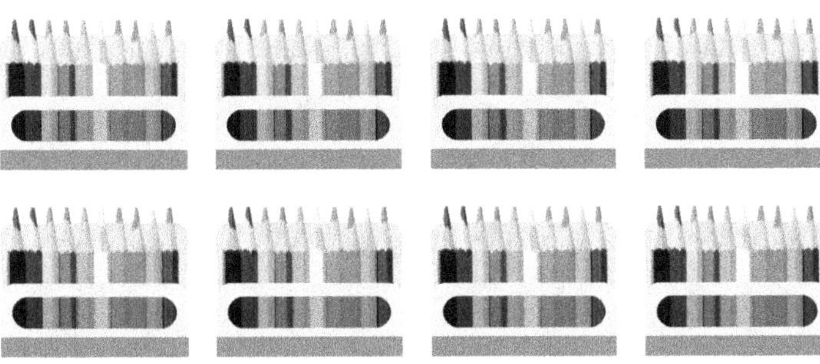
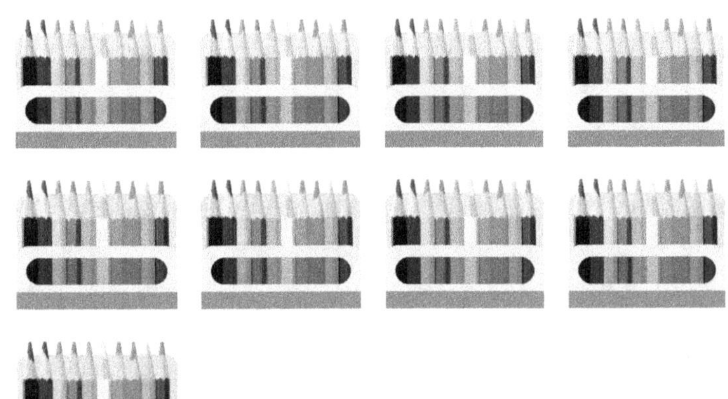

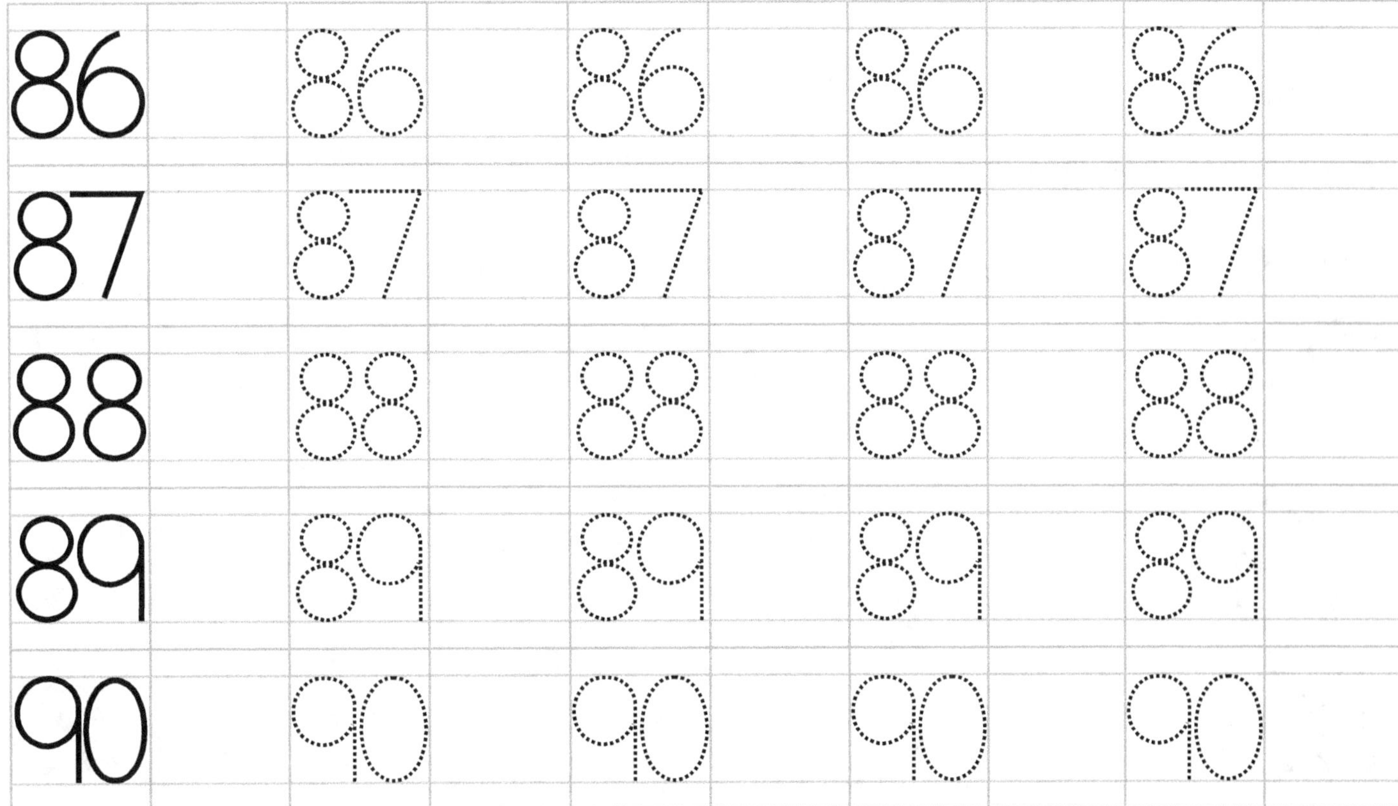

86	86	86	86	86
87	87	87	87	87
88	88	88	88	88
89	89	89	89	89
90	90	90	90	90

Date: ....   Teacher's signature: ....

Write the numbers from 71 to 80:

71   71
72   72
73   73
74   74
75   75
76   76
77   77
78   78
79   79
80   80

Date: ....

Teacher's signature: ....

Write the numbers from 81 to 90:

81

82

83

84

85

86

87

88

89

90

Date: ....

Teacher's signature: ....

91

NINETY ONE

TO

95

NINETY FIVE

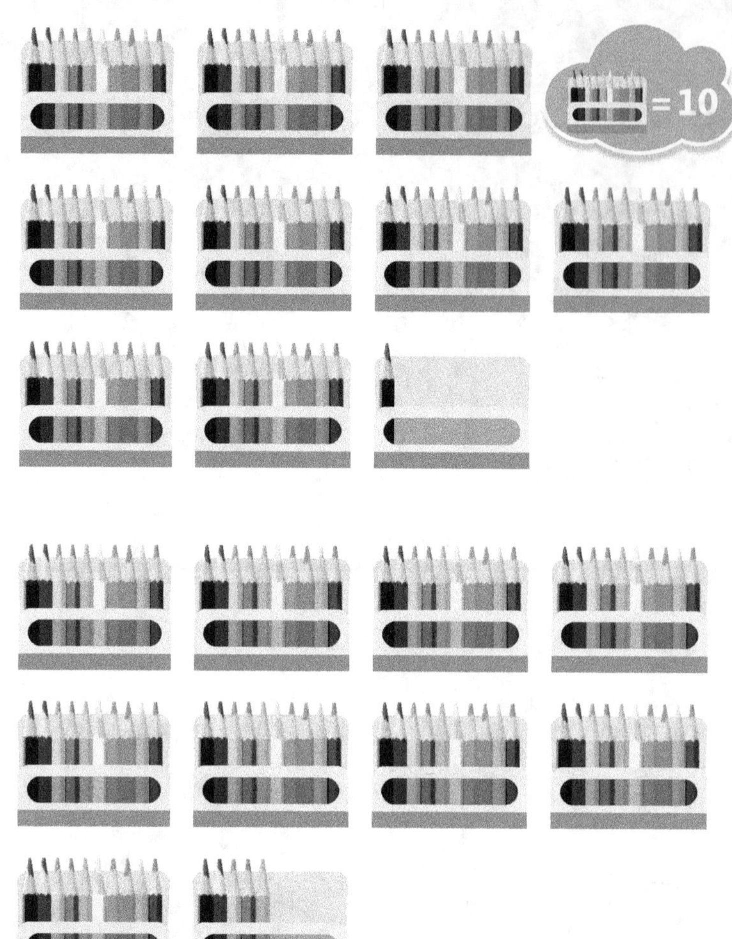

91	91	91	91	91
92	92	92	92	92
93	93	93	93	93
94	94	94	94	94
95	95	95	95	95

Date: ....

Teacher's signature: ....

96

NINETY-SIX

TO

100

HUNDRED

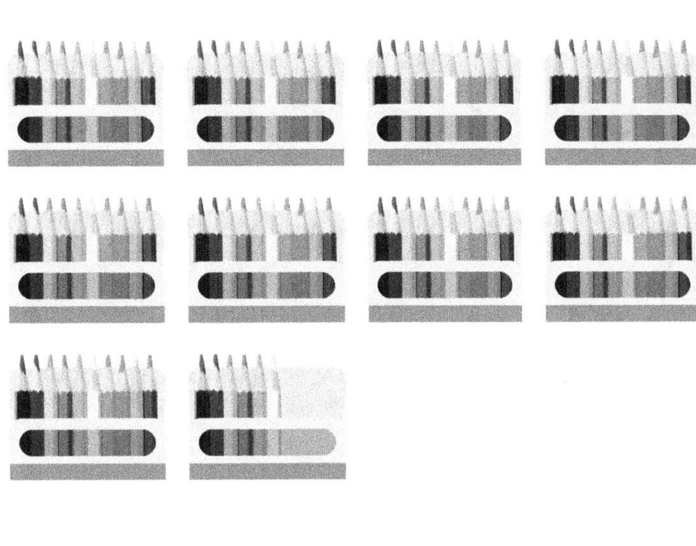

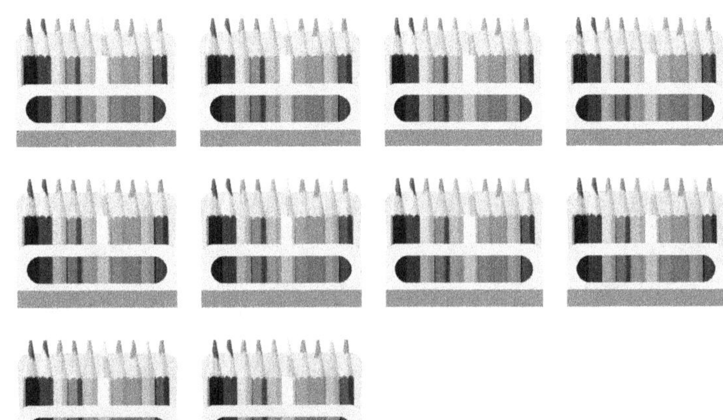

96	96	96	96	96
97	97	97	97	97
98	98	98	98	98
99	99	99	99	99
100	100	100	100	100

Date: ....

Teacher's signature: ....

91   91

92   92

93   93

94   94

95   95

96   96

97   97

98   98

99   99

100   100

Date: ....

Teacher's signature: ....

10 + 10 + 10 + 2 = 32

10 + 10 + 10 + 10 + 6 =

10 + 10 + 3 =

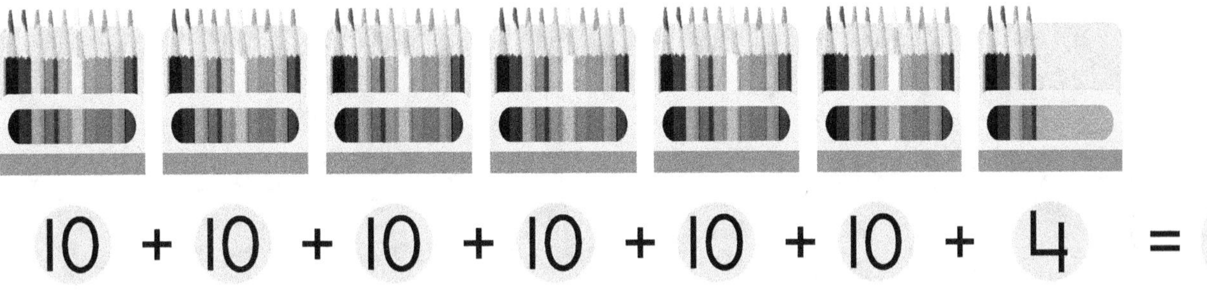

10 + 10 + 10 + 10 + 10 + 10 + 4 =

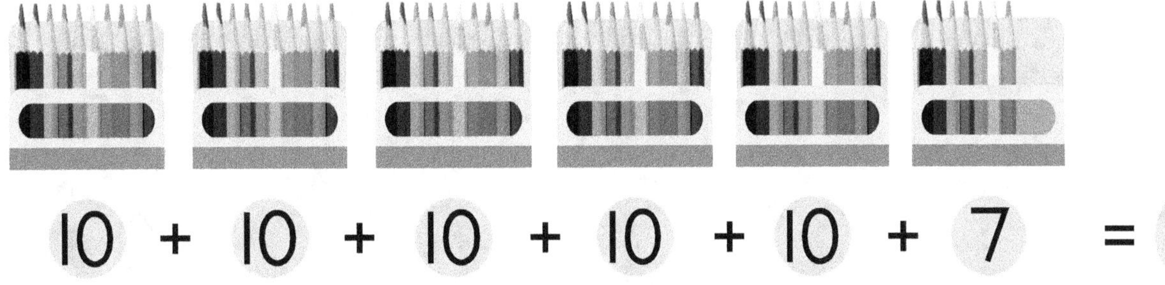

10 + 10 + 10 + 10 + 10 + 7 =

1									10
11									20
21									30
31									40
41									50
51									60
61									70
71									80
81									90
91									100

Date: ....

Teacher's signature: ....